This book belongs to

_____

THE TALE OF BENJAMIN BUNNY

BEATRIX POTTER
ILLUSTRATED BY
ALLEN ATKINSON

AN ARIEL BOOK

BANTAM BOOKS
TORONTO   NEW YORK   LONDON   SYDNEY   AUCKLAND

THE TALE OF BENJAMIN BUNNY
A Bantam Book
April 1983

Design: Iris Bass
Editorial Director: Ron Buehl
Senior Editor: Lu Ann Walther
Production: Hal Hochvert
Art Direction: Armand Eisen

ISBN 0-553-15203-3

Bantam Books are published by Bantam Books, Inc. Its trademark,
consisting of the words "Bantam Books" and the portrayal of a rooster, is
Registered in U.S. Patent and Trademark Office and in other countries.
Marca Registrada. Bantam Books, Inc., 666 Fifth Avenue, New York,
New York 10103

Printing and binding by
Printer, industria gráfica S.A   Provenza, 388   Barcelona-25
Depósito legal B. 40371-1983
PRINTED IN SPAIN
0 9 8 7 6 5 4

The art is dedicated
to Armand Eisen,
who saw more than I did

ONE MORNING A LITTLE
rabbit sat on a bank.

He pricked his ears and listened to the
trit-trot, trit-trot of a pony.

THE TALE OF BENJAMIN BUNNY

A gig was coming along the road; it
was driven by Mr. McGregor,
and beside him sat
Mrs. McGregor
in her best
bonnet.

THE TALE OF BENJAMIN BUNNY

As soon as they had passed, little Benjamin Bunny slid down into the road, and set off—with a hop, skip and a jump—to call upon his relations, who lived in the wood at the back of Mr. McGregor's garden.

THE TALE OF BENJAMIN BUNNY

That wood was full of rabbit holes; and in the neatest sandiest hole of all, lived Benjamin's aunt and his cousins— Flopsy, Mopsy, Cotton-tail and Peter.

THE TALE OF BENJAMIN BUNNY

Old Mrs. Rabbit was a widow; she earned her living by knitting rabbit-wool mittens and muffetees (I once bought a pair at a bazaar). She also sold herbs, and rosemary tea, and rabbit-tobacco (which is what *we* call lavender).

Little Benjamin did not very much want to see his Aunt.

THE TALE OF BENJAMIN BUNNY

THE TALE OF BENJAMIN BUNNY

THE TALE OF BENJAMIN BUNNY

He came round the back of the fir-tree, and nearly tumbled upon the top of his Cousin Peter.

Peter was sitting by himself. He looked poorly, and was dressed in a red cotton pocket-handkerchief.

"Peter"—said little Benjamin, in a whisper—"who has got your clothes?"

Peter replied—"The scare-crow in Mr. McGregor's garden," and described how he had been chased about the garden, and had dropped his shoes and coat.

Little Benjamin sat down beside his cousin, and assured him that Mr. McGregor had gone out in a gig, and Mrs. McGregor also; and certainly for the day, because she was wearing her best bonnet.

THE TALE OF BENJAMIN BUNNY

Peter said he hoped that it would rain.

At this point, old Mrs. Rabbit's voice was heard inside the rabbit hole, calling — "Cotton-tail! Cotton-tail! fetch some more camomile!"

Peter said he thought he might feel better if he went for a walk.

THE TALE OF BENJAMIN BUNNY

They went away hand in hand, and got upon the flat top of the wall at the bottom of the wood. From here they looked down into Mr. McGregor's garden. Peter's coat and shoes were plainly to be seen upon the scare-crow, topped with an old tam-o-shanter of Mr. McGregor's.

THE TALE OF BENJAMIN BUNNY

THE TALE OF BENJAMIN BUNNY

THE TALE OF BENJAMIN BUNNY

Little Benjamin said, "It spoils people's clothes to squeeze under a gate; the proper way to get in, is to climb down a pear-tree."

Peter fell down head first; but it was of no consequence, as the bed below was newly raked and quite soft.

THE TALE OF BENJAMIN BUNNY

It had been sown with lettuces.

They left a great many odd little foot-marks all over the bed, especially little Benjamin, who was wearing clogs.

THE TALE OF BENJAMIN BUNNY

Little Benjamin said that the first thing to be done was to get back Peter's clothes, in order that they might be able to use the pocket-handkerchief.

They took them off the scare-crow.

THE TALE OF BENJAMIN BUNNY

There had been rain during the night; there was water in the shoes, and the coat was somewhat shrunk.

THE TALE OF BENJAMIN BUNNY

Benjamin
tried on the
tam-o-shanter,
but it was too big
for him.

THE TALE OF BENJAMIN BUNNY

Then he suggested that they should fill the pocket-handkerchief with onions, as a little present for his Aunt.

Peter did not seem to be enjoying himself; he kept hearing noises.

THE TALE OF BENJAMIN BUNNY

Benjamin, on the contrary, was perfectly at home, and ate a lettuce leaf. He said that he was in the habit of coming to the garden with his father to get lettuces for their Sunday dinner.

THE TALE OF BENJAMIN BUNNY

(The name of little Benjamin's papa was old Mr. Benjamin Bunny.)

The lettuces certainly were very fine.

Peter did not eat anything; he said he should like to go home. Presently he dropped half the onions.

THE TALE OF BENJAMIN BUNNY

Little Benjamin said that it was not possible to get back up the pear-tree, with a load of vegetables.

THE TALE OF BENJAMIN BUNNY

He led the way boldly towards the other end of the garden. They went along a little walk on planks, under a sunny red-brick wall.

THE TALE OF BENJAMIN BUNNY

THE TALE OF BENJAMIN BUNNY

The mice sat on their door-steps cracking cherry-stones, they winked at Peter Rabbit and little Benjamin Bunny.

Presently Peter let the pocket-handkerchief go again.

THE TALE OF BENJAMIN BUNNY

THE TALE OF BENJAMIN BUNNY

THE TALE OF BENJAMIN BUNNY

They got amongst flower-pots, and frames and tubs; Peter heard noises worse than ever, his eyes were as big as lolly-pops!

He was a step or two in front of his cousin, when he suddenly stopped.

THE TALE OF BENJAMIN BUNNY

This is what those little rabbits saw round that corner!

THE TALE OF BENJAMIN BUNNY

THE TALE OF BENJAMIN BUNNY

Little Benjamin took one look, and then, in half a minute less than no time, he hid himself and Peter and the onions underneath a large basket....

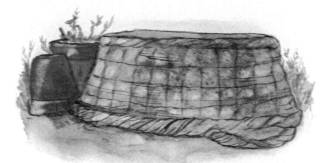

THE TALE OF BENJAMIN BUNNY

The cat got up and stretched herself,
and came and sniffed at the basket.
Perhaps she liked the smell of onions!

THE TALE OF BENJAMIN BUNNY

THE TALE OF BENJAMIN BUNNY

Anyway, she sat down upon the top of the basket.

She sat there for
five
hours.

THE TALE OF BENJAMIN BUNNY

*　*　*　*　*

I cannot draw you a picture of Peter and Benjamin underneath the basket, because it was quite dark, and because the smell of onions was fearful; it made Peter Rabbit and little Benjamin cry.

THE TALE OF BENJAMIN BUNNY

The sun got round behind the wood, and it was quite late in the afternoon; but still the cat sat upon the basket.

At length there was a pitter-patter, pitter-patter, and some bits of mortar fell from the wall above.

THE TALE OF BENJAMIN BUNNY

The cat looked up and saw old Mr. Benjamin Bunny prancing along the top of the wall of the upper terrace.

THE TALE OF BENJAMIN BUNNY

THE TALE OF BENJAMIN BUNNY

THE TALE OF BENJAMIN BUNNY

He was smoking a pipe of rabbit-tobacco, and had a little switch in his hand.

He was looking for his son.

THE TALE OF BENJAMIN BUNNY

Old Mr. Bunny had no opinion whatever of cats.

He took a tremendous jump off the top of the wall on to the top of the cat, and cuffed it off the basket, and kicked it into the green-house, scratching off a handful of fur.

The cat was too much surprised to scratch back.

THE TALE OF BENJAMIN BUNNY

THE TALE OF BENJAMIN BUNNY

THE TALE OF BENJAMIN BUNNY

When old Mr. Bunny had driven the cat into the green-house, he locked the door.

Then he came back to the basket and took out his son Benjamin by the ears, and whipped him with the little switch.

THE TALE OF BENJAMIN BUNNY

Then he took out his nephew Peter.

THE TALE OF BENJAMIN BUNNY

Then he took out the handkerchief of onions, and marched out of the garden.

THE TALE OF BENJAMIN BUNNY

When Mr. McGregor returned about half an hour later, he observed several things which perplexed him.

THE TALE OF BENJAMIN BUNNY

It looked as though some person had been walking all over the garden in a pair of clogs—only the foot-marks were too ridiculously little!

THE TALE OF BENJAMIN BUNNY

THE TALE OF BENJAMIN BUNNY

Also he could not understand how the cat could have managed to shut herself up *inside* the green-house, locking the door upon the *outside*.

THE TALE OF BENJAMIN BUNNY

When Peter got home, his mother forgave him, because she was so glad to see that he had found his shoes and coat. Cotton-tail and Peter folded up the pocket-handkerchief, and old Mrs. Rabbit strung up the onions and hung them from the kitchen ceiling, with the bunches of herbs and the rabbit-tobacco.

THE TALE OF BENJAMIN BUNNY